DADAJI'S PAINTBRUSH

RASHMI SIRDESHPANDE

RUCHI MHASANE

ANDERSEN PRESS

Once, in a tiny village in India,
there was a boy who loved to paint.
He lived with his grandfather in
an old house full of paintings.

This book belongs to:

....

In loving memory of my grandfather,
Shri Laxmikant Desai – R.S.

To Aaji-Abba and Aaji-Anna,
with whom I wish I had more time – R.M.

This paperback edition first published in 2023 by Andersen Press Ltd.

First published in Great Britain in 2022 by Andersen Press Ltd., 20 Vauxhall Bridge Road, London SW1V 2SA, UK • Vijverlaan 48, 3062 HL Rotterdam, Nederland

Text copyright © Rashmi Sirdeshpande 2022. Illustration copyright © Ruchi Mhasane 2022. The rights of Rashmi Sirdeshpande and Ruchi Mhasane to be identified

as the author and illustrator of this work have been asserted by them in accordance with the Copyright, Designs and Patents Act, 1988.

All rights reserved. Printed and bound in China.

1   3   5   7   9   10   8   6   4   2

British Library Cataloguing in Publication Data available. ISBN 978 1 83913 140 0

FSC
www.fsc.org
MIX
Paper from
responsible sources
FSC® C104723

First, the boy painted with his fingers. He printed with marigolds, betel leaves and coconut shells.

As he got bigger, he painted with brushes made of sticks with strips of cloth, reeds or jasmine flowers wrapped around the ends.

The village children would peep through the windows to watch them paint.

Sometimes, the boy's grandfather
would invite them to join in.

The boy and his grandfather did everything together.
They grew bananas, pineapples and jackfruit and
sold them in the local market...

shared sticky, juicy mangoes with the village children...

and made paper boats for them to float down the street in the monsoon rain. They read books and picked out what they'd paint the next day.

When the rains had gone, every night, they lay on their rooftop beds and watched the stars until they fell asleep.

They didn't have much but they had each other.

"Don't ever leave me," the boy would say.
"I won't," his grandfather would reply, holding
the boy so tight that his bones would hurt...

...but one day, he did.

All that was left of him was the old house
full of paintings. The boy stood at his
grandfather's desk.
He noticed a little box wrapped in string with a
note that read: "From Dadaji, with love."
Inside was his grandfather's best paintbrush.

At first, the boy didn't touch it. He couldn't.
He wouldn't. When he tried to look at it,
his chest ached.

Then, one day, he put it up on a shelf so
high he had to get up on his toes to reach it.

Days and months passed by.
Seasons changed.
The boy forgot all about the box.
At least, he tried to.

Mangoes didn't taste the
same anymore.
At night, the stars didn't
sparkle the way they used to.
And when the rains arrived
again, there was no one to
make paper boats with.

The village children didn't
visit anymore. The house
felt empty. Like the hole
in the boy's heart where
his grandfather used to
be. Where all the colours
used to be.

The boy took all the
paintings and locked them
away. In time, the paints
dried up and the box and
the paintings gathered dust.

Then, one day, a small girl turned up at the boy's door. She held a stick with reeds wrapped around the end.

"Please teach me how
to paint," she said.
"Like your dadaji
taught my mummy."

The boy shook his head but the girl
wouldn't leave. "Oh please," she said.

So he mixed up some
paints and found her a
fresh sheet of paper.

The girl plunged her brush
into the paints and dotted
the page with bright blue
and green splodges.
Then she stopped and
frowned.
"It's no good," she said.
"This was a bad idea. I
can't do it..."

She was about to give up when the boy said, "Wait..."
There was always a way.

He looked closely at the page. Then he remembered.
Then he smiled.

The boy unlocked the door at the back of the house and showed the girl his grandfather's paintings.

If they looked closely, in the background of every painting, they could see little splodges of paint. Sometimes made with fingers, sometimes with brushes made of sticks, reeds and flowers. Together, the boy and his grandfather had turned every one of them into something wonderful.

All it took was time and attention.

And so the boy reached for the box, took out his grandfather's paintbrush and started to paint.

The girl watched and copied. They painted
together every day and, as time passed by,
the house was filled with colour again.

The boy has been painting ever since.

Sometimes, the village children peep through the window to watch.
Sometimes they paint, they laugh, and the boy makes paper boats
for them to float away down the street in the monsoon rain.

He knows in his
heart that his
grandfather will
always be with him.

Author's note

This story is a blend of so many different things but at its heart, it's inspired by my love for my grandfather and his love for me. He didn't talk about it. He didn't have to. Whenever it was time for me to go back to England after visiting him in Goa, India, he would hold me so tight that my bones hurt. He isn't around anymore but that feeling that the people you love will always, always be with you – that's just how I feel.

There's so much in this book that I believe in. I believe there are no mistakes in art and that every single one of us should just feel free to play and create. I believe little things bring so much happiness – like sharing juicy mangoes or a story and watching the stars. And I believe love is something that lives on for ever and ever. I've put all of these things inside this little story and Ruchi has brought it to life in a way I could never have imagined. I love what we have created and I hope you will too.

Illustrator's note

Illustrating this book was both a joy and a challenge. The challenge was to show a colourful world of art in a setting that's already very vibrant, especially since I'm personally partial to muted palettes. The images, made with pencils and pastels, are built up on a number of papers using a lightbox, and combined digitally. This allowed me to play with the strength of the colours, especially in the scenes with the paintings.

It was a joy to illustrate because from the very first reading, Rashmi's words had evoked scenes from the western coastline of India that I'm so familiar with! Having grown up knowing the place, and being so fond of the people and culture where the story is set, it was a pleasure to bring it to life.